Great Big Animals

BIG BISON

By Ryan Nagelhout

Gareth Stevens
Publishing

Please visit our website, www.garethstevens.com. For a free color catalog of all our high-quality books, call toll free 1-800-542-2595 or fax 1-877-542-2596.

Library of Congress Cataloging-in-Publication Data

Nagelhout, Ryan.
Big bison / by Ryan Nagelhout.
  p. cm. — (Great big animals)
Includes index.
ISBN 978-1-4339-9421-0 (pbk.)
ISBN 978-1-4339-9422-7 (6-Pack)
ISBN 978-1-4339-9420-3 (library binding)
1. American bison – Juvenile literature. 2. Bison – Juvenile literature. I. Nagelhout, Ryan II. Title.
QL737.U53 N34 2013
599.643—dc23

First Edition

Published in 2014 by
Gareth Stevens Publishing
111 East 14th Street, Suite 349
New York, NY 10003

Editor: Ryan Nagelhout
Designer: Sarah Liddell

Photo credits: Cover, p. 1 Jean-Edouard Rozey/Shutterstock.com; p. 5 sergioboccardo/Shutterstock.com; pp. 7, 24 (fur) Igor Kovalenko/Shutterstock.com; pp. 9, 17 Holly Kuchera/Shutterstock.com; p. 11 Jonathan Tichon/Shutterstock.com; p. 13 Stan Osolinski/Oxford Scientific/Getty Images; pp. 15, 24 (horns) Milous/Shutterstock.com; p. 19 Bob Pool/Photographer's Choice RF/Getty Images; p. 21 Fotosearch/Getty Images; pp. 23, 24 (plains) Jim Parkin/Shutterstock.com.

Printed in the United States of America

CPSIA compliance information: Batch #CS13GS: For further information contact Gareth Stevens, New York, New York at 1-800-542-2595.

Contents

Bison are big animals!

They have lots of fur.

Big bison weigh
over 2,000 pounds.

They grow
over 6 feet tall!

They run very fast.
Some run up to
40 miles per hour.

13

They have two hard
spots on their heads.
These are horns.

Boys are called bulls.

Girls are called cows.

Words to Know

fur

horns

plains

Index

24

They live in big
flat places.
These are called plains.

They eat twigs
and grass.